This book is dedicated to Oklahoma educators. The OERB thanks you for your passion for teaching, your dedication to Oklahoma students and your continued support of energy education. Your work inspires us all.

OERB

Oklahoma Energy Resources Board

Created by the Oklahoma Legislature and energy industry leaders in 1993, the OERB is funded voluntarily by oil and natural gas producers and royalty owners through a one-tenth of 1 percent assessment on the sale of oil and natural gas. The OERB's purpose is to conduct environmental restoration of orphaned and abandoned well sites to educate Oklahomans about the vitality, contributions and environmental responsibility of Oklahoma's oil and natural gas industry.

Petro Pete's

BiG

BAD

Dream

Written by Carla Schaeperkoetter
Illustrated by Cameron Eagle

Copyright 2016 Oklahoma Energy Resources Board
www.oerb.com

Printed in Oklahoma, USA

ISBN 978-0-692-63684-8

It's nighttime in Petroville, Oklahoma and Petro Pete is in bed catching up on some reading.

"Repete, I didn't realize that so many items I use every day are made from oil and natural gas," said Pete.

Pete drifts off to sleep and wonders what
life would be like if we didn't have petroleum.

"Pete, it's time to wake up for school!" Pete's mom exclaimed as she knocked on his door.

Pete looked around the room and many of his belongings were missing, including his clothes for school.

"Repete! What did you do with my stuff?
Did you bury it again?" said Pete.

Repete shrugs his shoulders and shakes his head no.

Pete runs to the bathroom to brush his teeth and comb
his hair for school, but his toothbrush and comb are missing.

Pete shakes his head and doesn't know what to do.

"Pete! You better hurry up! You don't want to be late for school!" Pete's mom yells from the kitchen.

Pete heads outside in his pajamas to wait for the bus.

As the sun comes up, Pete realizes the bus driver must have forgotten about him. He thinks about taking his bike, but the tires are missing. Pete decides that he has to walk to school.

Pete gets to his classroom just in time.

"Pete, why are you wearing your
pajamas to school?" asked Sammy Shale.

"I've had a very strange morning. I think my dog buried all of my stuff. My clothes, toothbrush, comb and bike tires were all missing. And the bus driver forgot to pick me up!" replied Pete.

"Students, let's all take our seats. I think this is a good time to start science class. I might know what happened to all of Pete's belongings," said Mrs. Rigwell.

"Who can tell us what we learned about petroleum yesterday?" Mrs. Rigwell asked.

Nellie Johnstone raised her hand. "We talked about how petroleum is made from tiny sea creatures and plants that lived millions of years ago," said Nellie.

Patti raised her hand next. "We also learned about the tall metal derrick that is used to drill down to get to the petroleum, but I don't know what happens after that," said Patti.

"After the drilling rig drills down to the petroleum and the petroleum is pumped out of the ground, it is taken to a refinery and what do you think happens there?" asked Mrs. Rigwell as the school bell rang. "Oh, it's lunch time! Let's finish our lesson after recess."

"Let's play soccer on the playground today! I learned some new moves," said Sammy Shale.

"I'm going to get some ice cream before we go out there. I heard they have strawberry today!" exclaimed Pete.

Pete tries to fill his ice cream cone with strawberry ice cream, but it's coming out as milk. Pete is disappointed and decides to head to the playground instead.

"Pete, grab the soccer balls from the bin!" yelled Patti.

Pete walks over to the ball bin and finds it's empty.

"The soccer balls, basketballs and footballs are all missing!" Pete yells back to his friends. What happened to them? Pete wondered.

"Welcome back students! Time to get to work. Where did we leave off?" asked Mrs. Rigwell.

"You were saying that you thought Pete's missing things had to do with petroleum and a refinery, but how?" asked Sammy.

"Ah yes. Refineries take crude oil and separate it into parts to make different products. Once the crude oil is heated and separated, it can be used for many different purposes, like plastics, make-up, sneakers, and fuel," explained Mrs. Rigwell.

"Are you saying that my clothes, toothbrush, comb, bike tires and our soccer balls are all made from oil?" asked Pete.

"You are exactly right Pete. It sounds like you are missing all of your petroleum by-products today!" said Mrs. Rigwell.

"Even our soft serve ice cream machine wasn't working!" said Pete.

"I read the chemical they use to make the machine
freeze the milk is made from petroleum too," said Nellie.

"Great job students! I think we helped solve Pete's mystery," said Mrs. Rigwell.

"Sure did, but having no petroleum is like a nightmare!" said Pete just as the bell was ringing.

Pete is woken up by what sounds like a school bell, only he realizes it is his alarm clock. He springs up from bed and looks around the room and realizes that everything is back to normal. He looks at his calendar and gasps.

"Repete! That was all a dream! All of my petroleum by-products are back!" exclaimed Pete.

Repete shook his head and gave Pete a thumbs up.